Mermaids Don't
Run Track

To: Zoe
From: Zoe
To: PJ
From: PJ

ISBN-13: 978-0-590-84906-7
ISBN-10: 0-590-84906-9

Text copyright © 1997 by Marcia Thornton Jones and Debra S. Dadey.
Illustrations copyright © 1997 by Scholastic Inc.
All rights reserved. Published by Scholastic Inc. SCHOLASTIC, APPLE PAPERBACKS, THE ADVENTURES OF THE BAILEY SCHOOL KIDS, and associated logos are trademarks and/or registered trademarks of Scholastic Inc.

34 33 32 31   11 12/0

Printed in the U.S.A.   40

This edition first printing, July 2007

Book design by Laurie Williams

Mermaids Don't Run Track

by Debbie Dadey
and
Marcia Thornton Jones

illustrated by John Steven Gurney

Scholastic Inc.

New York Toronto London Auckland Sydney
Mexico City New Delhi Hong Kong Buenos Aires

To Tina O'Neal and her daughters Candice and Brenna—DD
For Judy Minnehan—a good friend who knows the value of coaching with a song and a smile!—MTJ

1

Throw Your Teacher Overboard

"Row, row, row your boat, gently down the stream. Throw your teacher overboard and listen to her scream," Eddie and Howie sang at the top of their lungs.

Liza pushed her blonde hair out of her face and turned to look at Eddie and Howie. "Instead of singing, why don't you concentrate on how we can win the track meet?" she asked them.

The third-graders from Bailey Elementary were on their way to nearby Camp Lone Wolf for a district-wide track meet. They would have three days to practice at the camp before the meet. They were even supposed to have a special track coach to help them train.

Eddie grinned at Liza. "Don't worry.

1

With me on the Bailey School team, we're sure to beat the Sheldon Sharks."

Eddie pushed his baseball cap down over his red curly hair and started singing again. Liza's friend Melody groaned when Howie joined in with, "Throw your teacher overboard and . . ."

Eddie and Howie didn't stop singing as their bus bounced over a big bump in the gravel driveway. Liza put her hand on Melody's arm and smiled. "Don't worry. We're almost there. Then we won't have to listen to them sing anymore."

Melody clapped when she saw the big sign that said, WELCOME TO CAMP LONE WOLF: A HOME FOR EVERY PLANT AND CREATURE. "I never thought I'd be glad to see that again," Melody said.

"I never thought we'd live to see it again," Liza whispered. Both girls nodded. The first time they had gone to Camp Lone Wolf, they had been sure that the camp director, Mr. Jenkins, was a

3

werewolf. As a matter of fact, they *still* thought he was a werewolf.

"Let's just stay as far away from Mr. Jenkins as possible," Melody told Liza. "As long as we stay away from him, we should be perfectly safe. After all, there's nothing else to be afraid of."

"I hope you're right," Liza said as the bus jerked to a stop right beside a very hairy man. It was Mr. Jenkins. When he saw Liza looking out the window, he smiled so wide his pointy eyeteeth showed. Then Mr. Jenkins threw back his head and howled.

2

Staying Alive

"Welcome to Camp Lone Wolf," Mr. Jenkins bellowed as the kids hopped off the bus. "I'd like to introduce you to Miss Waterford, your special track coach. She's going to help you train for the meet on Sunday."

The third-graders stared at Miss Waterford. A seashell comb pulled her long shiny blonde hair away from her face.

"She looks like a model," Melody whispered.

Liza nodded. "Or a princess from a fairy tale."

Howie stopped staring at Miss Waterford long enough to look at Eddie. "I think Eddie's in love," Howie teased.

Eddie turned red. "I'm just trying to

figure out what someone so pretty has to do with a track meet."

Miss Waterford greeted the third-graders with a huge smile and a voice like music. "I am thrilled to be a part of the first annual Lone Wolf Track Meet. Running is very special to me. I value it more than sunken treasure."

Eddie couldn't believe his ears. "Nothing is more valuable than sunken treasure," he whispered.

After the Bailey School Kids put their bags in their cabins, they met Miss Waterford at the flagpole.

"Follow me to the track," Miss Waterford said. She jogged down a dirt path to a brand-new racing track. The third-graders ran after her with Mr. Jenkins trotting behind.

Miss Waterford blew on a large conch shell to begin the run. The kids raced around and around the big circle. Before long, Howie felt dizzy. "I think I'm a little too warmed up now," Howie told Miss Waterford.

Liza nodded. "Can't we stop? I'm tired of running."

Miss Waterford jogged in place to answer. "I never get tired of running," she said. "I love the feel of my sneakers hitting the ground. It's like music to me."

"How can running in circles be music?" Eddie asked.

Miss Waterford smiled. "Listen, and you will hear it." She made the kids get in a circle and jog in place. Soon, their sneakers starting hitting the track at the same time. It sounded like a distant war drum.

"Now, all we need are some words," Miss Waterford said. "And we'll be making our own victory music. Follow me!"

Miss Waterford started jogging around the track. All the Bailey School Kids followed. In a clear voice she sang words to go with their steps.

Bailey School Kids run all day,
Getting faster all the way.
'Round this track we'll run again,
This way we are sure to win.

All the kids were singing with her. Before they realized it, they had circled the track four more times.

"That was great," Liza said. She was barely even panting.

Melody nodded. "Miss Waterford's song helped me forget how tired I was."

Miss Waterford touched the seashell comb in her hair and nodded. "You have worked hard. Perhaps you would like to cool off by wading in the lake."

"All right!" Eddie cheered.

The kids ran to their cabins to change into swimming suits. Melody was the first one ready. Liza, Howie, and Eddie were close behind. "Race you to the water!" Melody yelled. Melody ran fast, but Miss Waterford easily zipped past her.

The Bailey School Kids were sure Miss Waterford would beat them into the water, but just before they reached the dock, Miss Waterford skidded to a stop. Melody almost ran right into her.

"Is something wrong?" Melody asked.

"I don't want to jump in the water," she told Melody. "I'm not ready to stop running."

And then Miss Waterford dashed back up the trail and out of sight.

"I'm worried about Miss Waterford," Melody said.

"You should be worried," Eddie said. "We should all worry. But not about Miss Waterford."

"What do you mean?" Liza asked.

Eddie pointed a trembling finger at the lake. "I mean, we'd better worry about getting out of here alive!"

3

Crazy Idea

Melody, Howie, and Liza looked where Eddie pointed. What they saw sent shivers scooting down their backs.

Mr. Jenkins stood in the center of the dock reading a piece of paper. He wore ragged swimming trunks and the silver dog tags hanging around his neck sparkled in the sun. But that's not what the kids stared at. Mr. Jenkins was the hairiest person they had ever seen. He had hair on his chest, hair on his arms, and hair on his legs. He even had hair on his knuckles. He looked like a wolf standing on two legs.

Mr. Jenkins looked up from the paper he was reading and smiled. The kids

couldn't help noticing his pointy canine teeth.

"I was so busy reading I didn't hear you," Mr. Jenkins barked.

"I thought wolves and dogs could hear anything," Melody whispered, but she stopped talking when Mr. Jenkins looked straight at her.

Mr. Jenkins carefully put the piece of paper under a big towel so the wind wouldn't blow it away. "Come on in," he said with a grin. And then Mr. Jenkins jumped into the cold waters of Lake Erin.

The rest of the Bailey School Kids jumped in after him. But Eddie pulled Melody and Howie by the arm. Liza followed close behind.

"What do you think Mr. Jenkins was reading?" he asked.

Howie shrugged. "It's none of our business," he told his friend.

"It wouldn't hurt if we took a look," Eddie said. Before they could stop him,

Eddie darted over to Mr. Jenkins' towel and snatched the paper. The four kids huddled over it.

The picture was an advertisement torn from a sailing magazine. It showed a huge wooden ship with pillow-white sails billowing from the tall masts. Cracked yellow paint on its side spelled out the name *Mermaid Maiden*.

"What a neat boat," Eddie said.

Howie pointed to the letters on the side of the ship. "It's not a boat. It's a sailing ship called the *Mermaid Maiden!*"

"But a ship is a boat, isn't it, Mr. Smartypants?" Eddie asked with his hands on his hips.

Howie didn't get to answer because just then a huge shadow fell over them.

"It's my dream," a deep voice growled.

"*AAAAH!*" Howie, Melody, and Liza screamed together. Eddie ducked behind Melody. They all stared up into the dripping whiskers of Mr. Jenkins.

Mr. Jenkins grabbed the paper from

15

Eddie's hands. "I've always wanted to sail the seven seas under the light of a full moon, listening to the song of the ocean," he said. "According to this advertisement, I can afford to do it."

Eddie held up his hand. "Don't get mad, but don't you think that's a crazy idea?"

"I think it's a great idea," Liza said. "My parents went on a cruise once. They said it was so romantic."

Eddie rolled his eyes. "Oh, brother!"

"Coach Waterford found this advertisement. She's not only a great coach, she's an expert sailor." Mr. Jenkins handed the paper to Liza. "Coach Waterford thinks buying the *Mermaid Maiden* is a great idea. And you kids will be the first to get a ride," Mr. Jenkins boomed. "But until then, let's swim!"

Mr. Jenkins took a running leap off the short dock. When his head popped up, he looked just like a wet dog. Melody,

Howie, and Eddie watched as he dog-paddled away from shore.

But Liza never took her eyes off the ship picture.

"Oh my gosh!" she gasped.

4

Barrel of Slugs

"I think Mr. Jenkins is in big trouble!" Liza said. Howie, Melody, Liza, and Eddie were still standing on the dock. Liza hadn't stopped staring at the ship picture.

"No, we're the ones in trouble," Melody said. "I thought Mr. Jenkins would crunch us like doggy biscuits when he saw us looking at his stuff."

Howie nodded. "We had no business looking at his picture. You'd better put it back under his towel."

"I'm not putting it back until you take a good look at it," Liza said firmly.

Eddie rolled his eyes before glancing at the picture. "Okay, it's a ship. Can we swim now?"

"No, look closer," Liza said. Melody, Howie, and Eddie stared hard at the picture. Eddie shrugged and played with the string on his bathing suit.

"Don't you see it?" Liza asked.

"I see that everybody else is having fun in the water and I'm sweat city," Eddie said.

"I see it now!" Melody screeched. "The carving on the ship looks like a mermaid."

The four friends peered closer. The photograph clearly showed a beautiful carving of a woman with flowing hair on the front of the ship. Where her legs should have been was a long scaly fish tail. The tail ended with two huge flippers.

"That's not unusual," Howie told them. "Old sailing ships often had mermaids carved on them. They're called figureheads. I saw it on *Educational TV.*"

"Yuck! You actually watch that junk?" Eddie asked.

Howie nodded. "I like it. Sometimes I even learn stuff."

Eddie groaned and looked at the kids playing in the water. Melody stared at the picture. "The mermaid is beautiful," she said. "Like a model."

Liza nodded so hard her long blonde ponytail flipped over the top of her head. "Or a princess from a fairy tale," she said.

Melody gasped. "It can't be," she whispered.

"It is," Liza said softly. "That mermaid is our very own Coach Waterford."

Eddie threw back his head and laughed. "Then I'm Rudolph the Red-nosed Reindeer."

Melody looked at Eddie and giggled. "Well, your nose *is* a little red. Exactly where were you last Christmas?"

"Ha, ha," Eddie said. "You're both as funny as a barrel of slugs. But you still haven't told us what a mermaid would be doing at Camp Lone Wolf."

"That's why Mr. Jenkins is in trouble," Liza explained as she put the ship picture back under Mr. Jenkins' towel. "Miss Waterford likes running, remember?"

Howie, Melody, and Eddie nodded. "Well," Liza said, "there's only one way a mermaid can stay human and keep running. She has to get a mortal man to go to sea forever."

"Where did you hear that?" Howie asked.

"I watch TV, too," Liza said.

"What mortal man are you talking about?" Melody asked.

Liza didn't say a word. Instead, she stared out over the water at Mr. Jenkins.

5

Dead Ringer

"You're forgetting one important thing," Eddie said with a grin. "Mermaids don't run track. They can't because they have no legs. And in case you didn't notice, Coach Waterford has two very long and very fast legs."

"Eddie's right," Howie said as the four kids walked onto the dock.

"But you have to admit Coach Waterford is a dead ringer for that mermaid," Liza said.

"And you're a dead ringer for an octopus sucker," Eddie laughed.

Before anyone could stop her, Liza reached out and gave Eddie a shove. Eddie teetered on the edge of the dock, his arms flapping like a seagull's wings.

"Oh, no!" he squealed.

Eddie fell into the chilly water with one giant splash. Liza and Melody giggled.

"I'll get you for that!" Eddie sputtered as he thrashed on top of the water. Then he used his hand to splash his three friends.

Howie cannonballed into the lake to help Eddie. Together, they sent water sailing through the air. In just minutes, the girls were soaked and giant puddles dotted the dock.

Liza wrung out her ponytail. "You'd better stop that," she warned.

Melody just giggled and jumped into the water.

"Hey!" Liza yelled. "You're supposed to be on my side."

Melody yelled back. "But being in the water is fun!"

"Not to some people," a voice answered from the path leading to the dock.

Melody, Howie, and Eddie floated in the water while Liza turned to face Coach Waterford. The coach stood in the shadows of nearby trees, several yards away from the wet dock. Liza stared at Coach Waterford's feet, but the rest of her friends didn't notice.

"Aren't you going to go for a swim?" Howie called to the coach. "The water feels great after that hot workout you put us through."

Coach Waterford smiled, but then she shook her head. When she talked, her voice rose and fell like the notes to a lullaby. "The cool water can be a magic potion after a good run. But not for me. The water mixed with sun makes my skin dry and scaly. I prefer to stay in the shade."

"Then I'll help cool you off!" Eddie offered. He splashed a huge wave of water straight at Coach Waterford.

"NO!" Coach Waterford pierced the air with an opera-singer scream and raced

back up the path just as water splattered on the dirt. Coach Waterford ran so fast she looked like a blur passing through the shadows of the forest. In a blink she was gone.

"Wow!" Howie laughed. "I'll bet she could win every race at the next Olympic games. All they'd have to do is threaten to splash her."

Eddie laughed. "Our coach may be an expert runner, but she sure is strange when it comes to a few drops of water."

"Not strange," Liza said, "for a mermaid!"

6

Mermaid's Curse

Melody, Howie, and Eddie kicked over to the dock and clung to the ladder.

"Now what are you talking about?" Eddie asked.

Liza glanced over her shoulder to make sure Coach Waterford wasn't spying on them. Then she sat down on the dock's edge, leaning over so she could whisper to her friends in the water. "Everybody knows that water is a mermaid's curse."

"Curse?" Melody asked. "I thought mermaids needed the water. Like a fish needs water."

"And like Liza needs a brain," Eddie added.

Liza ignored Eddie. "Mermaids breathe

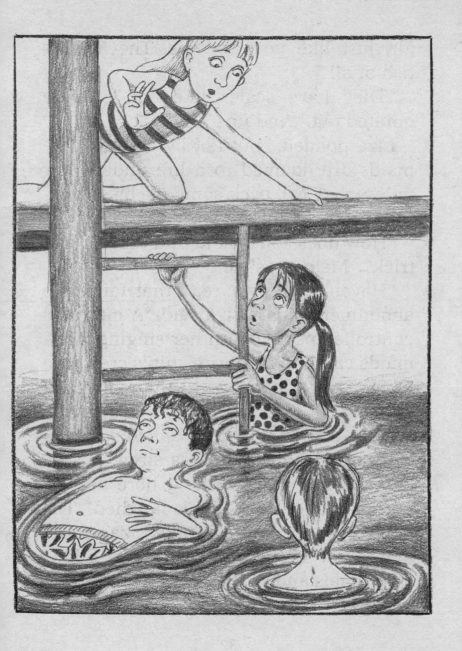

air, just like you and me. They're not fish at all."

"They have scales like fish," Howie pointed out. "And fins."

Liza nodded. "But not by choice. Mermaids are doomed to a life underwater unless they can trick someone by switching the curse onto them."

"How does a mermaid pull that kind of trick?" Melody asked.

"Haven't you ever read that fairy tale about mermaids?" Liza said. "A mermaid controlled people with her singing. Mermaids can lure an entire ship's crew into dangerous waters with their magical voices."

"Like a siren?" Melody asked.

Liza nodded. "Just like a siren."

"The only sirens around here are the ones on police cars," Eddie laughed. "The ones that are coming to take Liza away!"

"I'm not kidding," Liza warned Eddie. "Mermaids and sirens are sea fairies that have lured sailors with their singing for centuries. It's the only way they can change their fish tails into legs. And that's exactly what I think Coach Waterford is doing to Mr. Jenkins."

Eddie laughed so hard he sputtered the water in front of him into little bubbles. "If you ask me," Eddie said, "we'd be doing Bailey City a favor by getting rid of Mr. Jenkins. Who would miss a werewolf, anyway?"

"All the animals here at Camp Lone Wolf," Liza explained. "Without Mr. Jenkins, there would be no Camp Lone Wolf and all the creatures would have to find somewhere else to live."

Howie tried not to hurt Liza's feelings. "Just because our track coach looks like the figurehead on a boat doesn't mean she's a mermaid."

"Howie's right," Melody said gently. "Coach Waterford is just an ordinary lady who likes to run."

"A plain ordinary lady with huge feet?" Liza asked.

"What do her feet have to do with being a mermaid?" Howie asked.

Liza looked down at her friends. "You were too busy acting like drowning dolphins to notice. Coach Waterford has very unusual feet. They're at least two times bigger than most feet, and four times wider. They look just like fins!"

"That's probably from all the running she does," Howie explained.

"Her feet didn't get that way from running," Liza said. "And I think we should tell Mr. Jenkins before it's too late."

"Then you'll be sticking your own big feet right in your very big mouth," Howie warned.

"I think Liza's idea is all wet," Eddie interrupted. "But not wet enough!" Eddie's hand shot out of the water and grabbed Liza's wrists, pulling her into the waters of Lake Erin.

7

Night Music

The campfire cast eerie shadows on the trees, and Liza shivered in the cool night air. The Bailey runners huddled around the fire roasting marshmallows. Mr. Jenkins sat at the very edge of the ring of firelight. Mr. Jenkins never sat near the fire. Some of the campers were sure it was because werewolves are deathly afraid of fire.

Eddie peeled sticky marshmallow from his fingers. "I could eat a whole bag of these," he said.

"Too much sugar isn't good for you," Howie warned.

"But sugar gives you energy," a big kid named Huey said. "And we need our energy for tomorrow. Coach Waterford said we have a lot of work ahead of us if we plan on beating the Sheldon Sharks this Friday."

A few kids nodded. They all started talking at once about how hard it would be to beat the best team around.

The fire had nearly died down when they first heard the noise. It started out low, like wind whining through pine trees. But then it grew louder and louder. All the campers stopped talking so they could listen to the crystal-clear voice singing through the night air.

"Who would be singing at this time of night?" Howie whispered.

"I know," Liza said. "It's the mermaid trying to lure Mr. Jenkins away from camp."

"I think she's already lured your brain away," Eddie laughed.

"Where *is* Coach Waterford?" Melody asked.

"I haven't seen her since this afternoon," Howie said.

"That's strange," Eddie said. "She didn't even eat dinner with us."

Liza shrugged. "Most mermaids don't care for cooked fish," she mumbled just loud enough for her closest friends to hear. "She's probably down at the water, gobbling raw bass and catfish."

"*Shhh,*" Melody warned. "Do you want everybody to think you've gone bonkers?"

But Liza didn't have to worry. None of the other third-graders was listening. They all stared silently into the glowing embers of the fire, wearing silly grins. A few of them hummed along with the strange singing.

"Everybody looks like they're sleeping with their eyes open," Eddie said.

"Maybe they are," Liza said. "Especially Mr. Jenkins."

The four friends looked at Mr. Jenkins.

He stared dreamily into the fire, swaying to the sound of the mysterious song. He sighed and then yawned so wide they saw his eyeteeth.

"Time for bed!" Mr. Jenkins said when the strange song ended. "You'll need plenty of rest between now and Friday. Coach Waterford tells me those Sharks are real terrors of the track."

"She would know about sharks," Liza muttered.

"*Shhh,*" Howie and Melody said at the same time.

Mr. Jenkins kicked sand on the fire until it sputtered out. The campers clicked on flashlights and headed toward their cabins. Howie, Melody, Liza, and Eddie trailed behind the rest of the third-graders.

But just as Mr. Jenkins turned down the path to his cabin, the eerie singing floated over their heads again. Mr. Jenkins stopped dead in his tracks. "Everyone in their bunks!" he bellowed. Then, slowly, he turned.

Liza gulped as Mr. Jenkins started down the black night path that led straight to the water's edge.

8

Fairy Tale

"I wish whoever is doing that singing would put a sock in it," Eddie complained in the boys' cabin. "I'm trying to get some sleep."

Howie put his pillow over his head to block out the sound. "Whatever happened to peace and quiet in the woods?"

"It is peaceful, except for that stupid singing," Eddie snapped and threw his pillow at the window.

Over in Cabin Gray Wolf, the girls were having the same problem. "I wish that singing would stop. It's driving me nuts," Melody told Liza.

Liza pulled the covers off her head and nodded. "That's exactly what it's supposed to do."

Melody peered down from her top bunk. "What are you talking about?"

Liza sighed and pulled the covers back over her head. "Try to get some sleep. I'll tell you in the morning." Liza tossed and turned for half an hour. Right before she fell asleep, she was sure she heard howling along with the strange singing.

The next morning at breakfast, all the kids had dark circles under their eyes. "I'm too tired to eat," Melody said with a yawn.

"I'm going to complain to Mr. Jenkins about all that singing," Eddie said as he buttered a piece of toast.

Howie shook his head. "You'd better not. He'll probably start his werewolf howl right along with the crazy singing. Before I fell asleep, I heard Mr. Jenkins howling."

"I did, too," Liza said. "And that's just the beginning. I know that was Coach Waterford singing and she's not going to

stop until she has Mr. Jenkins under her control."

"You're nuttier than a pecan tree," Eddie said. He made a circling motion with his finger beside his head.

"Eddie's right," Howie said. "Even if Coach Waterford *is* a mermaid, why would she want to control a hairy camp director like Mr. Jenkins?"

"I told you," Liza said. "So she can keep her legs forever."

"That's crazy!" Eddie said. "Coach Waterford isn't a mermaid and I can prove it tonight!"

9

Howling at the Moon

Howie sang as loudly as he could when the third-graders did sit-ups. A group of girls chanted Miss Waterford's victory song as they ran around the track. In fact, everybody was singing that morning. Everyone except Eddie.

"Didn't they hear enough singing last night?" Eddie complained.

"It is weird," Melody said. "The louder we sing, the faster we run."

"Maybe we should sing really loud when we race against the Sheldon Sharks," Howie said with a smile.

"Maybe we can get flying fish to race against the Sheldon Sharks," Eddie said.

"Do you know where we can get some?" Howie joked. "We need all the help we can get."

"I'll help you tonight when I prove that all this talk about magic and mermaids is a bunch of mustard-covered bologna," Eddie said.

Just then, Coach Waterford led a group of third-graders past the four friends. All the runners were singing.

"The Sheldon Sharks will eat you alive," Coach Waterford yelled, "unless you get up and practice."

Melody, Liza, Howie, and Eddie stopped talking and jogged with the rest of the third-graders. Then they ran and practiced relays. By the end of the day, they were tired and sore. But they were much faster.

After dinner, the four friends huddled at the water's edge. "All we have to do is wait and watch," Eddie explained.

"The only thing I want to watch is the inside of my eyelids," Melody said. "I'm pooped from all that running."

Howie rubbed his legs. "I know how

you feel. I'm exhausted and the big race with the Sheldon Sharks is tomorrow."

"You're the ones who think Coach Waterford is a mermaid," Eddie said. "If we see her turn into a mermaid and start singing, then we'll have proof. But keep your eyes open. I plan to prove that Coach Waterford is just some kind of crazy lady who likes to run and sing."

"I don't think this will work," Liza said. "Coach Waterford —"

"Don't worry," Eddie interrupted. "This will work."

"I hope we prove something soon," Melody said, yawning. "Before I fall asleep."

The singing did start again, but the kids didn't hear it. They were sound asleep on the shore of Lake Erin. It was something else that woke them. Something loud.

In the distance, they heard the eerie singing they had heard the night before.

But it was a wolf howling at the moon that scared them worse. And it wasn't far away.

Howie sat up and rubbed his eyes. "Look," he gasped. "It's the wolf!"

His friends looked into the deep shadows where he pointed. Just then, a huge animal crashed through a nearby bush.

"Oh, great," Melody squealed softly. "If the mermaid doesn't get us, the werewolf will! We're doomed!"

"Let's get out of here, before it's too late," Howie hissed.

"*Run!*" Eddie said. But he didn't need to tell his friends what to do. They were already halfway up the hill to the cabins.

10

Fortune-telling

The next morning at breakfast the kids were more tired than ever. Liza was so sleepy she laid her face onto her plate.

"I'm afraid the Sheldon Sharks are going to eat us alive," Howie said, looking at Liza.

"Singing may be our only hope," Melody said softly.

Liza raised up her face. Powdered sugar from her donut covered her nose. "I'd be happy if I never heard anyone sing ever again," she said before putting her head back down.

"I did notice something about the singing," Melody told them.

"Me, too," Eddie snapped. "I noticed it was very annoying, just like you."

Melody ignored Eddie and went on. "It wasn't coming from the lake. It was coming from the counselors' cabins."

"That proves it," Eddie said. "Coach Waterford is just a regular person."

Liza lifted her sugar-covered face again. "That doesn't prove anything. I tried to tell you last night. Mermaids don't —"

"*Shhh*," Howie warned. "It's Coach Waterford."

Coach Waterford put her hand on Liza's shoulder and smiled at the group. She was so pretty, even Eddie had to smile back. "Today is the day," Coach Waterford said. "We're going to beat the Sheldon Sharks."

Eddie shook his head. "We're so tired, we couldn't beat a turtle with heat stroke."

Coach Waterford touched the seashell comb in her hair and laughed. Her laugh sounded like wind chimes tinkling in the wind. "I know that you will do *very* well against the Sheldon team," she said firmly.

Coach Waterford smiled again and walked quickly away. The rest of the kids ate their breakfast, but Liza stared after the coach. Eddie gave Liza a shove and asked, "Hey, dust face, what's wrong with you?"

"Mermaids can tell the future," Liza whispered softly. "Coach Waterford is not only a coach and a great singer — she's also a fortune-teller."

"So what?" Melody said.

"So, she really *is* a mermaid," Liza whispered.

Eddie shrugged. "Right now, I don't care if she's the Queen of the Sea. I just hope she's right about beating the Sharks."

The whistle blew to start the races and the kids rushed out to the track. The Sheldon Sharks were huge in their gray

track uniforms. But it didn't matter; the Bailey team managed to win the first five races.

Eddie panted after winning first place in the fifty-yard dash. "It looks like Coach Waterford is right about us winning."

Liza sat on the ground to rest. "I've been thinking about Coach Waterford," she said.

Eddie rolled his eyes. "Not more mermaid stuff again. Can't I just enjoy the races?"

Liza pointed her finger at Eddie. "If it wasn't for Mr. Jenkins, we wouldn't even be having these races," she told him.

"Liza's right," Melody said. "Mr. Jenkins invited us here."

"And he's made Camp Lone Wolf into a safe home for animals," Howie said.

Liza sniffed. "And now a mermaid is going to force him out to sea. We have to save him!"

11

Victory Song

The late afternoon sun beat down on the Camp Lone Wolf running track. The score was tied. Both teams were resting in the shade.

"How did we let the Sharks catch up to us?" Melody wailed.

"We were doing great in the first half," Howie agreed. "Then we let the Sharks take over."

"There's only one event left," Eddie groaned. "If we don't win that, we've lost the entire track meet."

"We should be concentrating on saving Mr. Jenkins," Liza said.

Coach Waterford blew on the conch shell for the team to gather around her.

"I thought you said we'd win today," Eddie said.

Coach Waterford adjusted the seashell comb in her hair and smiled. "Keep a song in your heart. I'm sure you'll win."

"But we're too tired to run another race," Melody mumbled as the Bailey runners prepared for the relay. "The Sheldon Sharks are just too tough for us."

"We have to try," Howie said.

Melody, Liza, and Eddie nodded. Then they jogged to their places and got ready for the whistle to start the relay race.

Just then, the kids heard a soft tune being hummed, coming from the bleachers. A few Bailey runners joined along with the tune, and soon it grew louder and louder. Everyone was singing the Bailey School victory song. The runners from the Sheldon team stared at Coach Waterford. Just then the whistle blew.

Howie darted from the starting line and was halfway to Melody before the Sheldon team knew what had happened. By the time Howie handed off his baton to Melody, the Sheldon Sharks were so far behind, they didn't stand a chance.

Melody couldn't resist breaking into song as she tore around the track and handed off the baton to Eddie. "Go!" she sang after him.

Liza held out her hand, ready to grab the baton as soon as Eddie slapped it into her palm. While she waited, she listened to all the voices blending together into one loud song. Even Eddie's voice croaked louder and louder as he raced toward her.

The entire team was at the finish line to see Liza beat the Sheldon Sharks' runner. Everyone crowded around as Mr. Jenkins proudly presented the very first ever Camp Lone Wolf Track Meet trophy to the Bailey runners.

"We didn't win this trophy by ourselves," Howie told the others. "We would have lost without Coach Waterford's victory song!"

"That's right!" Eddie said. "Let's hear it for Coach Waterford!"

Coach Waterford blushed as the Bailey runners cheered.

"I don't care if she is a mermaid," Melody whispered to her friend Liza. "I think Coach Waterford is wonderful!"

Liza grabbed Melody's arm. "Don't you see what she's done?"

12

The End of Camp Lone Wolf

"You can't still believe she's a mermaid," Howie said. "After all, she just helped us win the track meet!"

"Exactly," Liza said. "And she did it with magical singing." It was later in the afternoon and the Bailey runners were wading off the shores of Lake Erin.

"So what if she did?" Eddie said. "She's kind of like the Pied Piper. As a matter of fact, she could come in real handy when school starts. Maybe we could get her to get rid of all the teachers in Bailey City!"

"Just like she'll be luring Mr. Jenkins away from camp," Liza said. "It will be the end of Camp Lone Wolf without Mr. Jenkins to take care of the animals."

"Liza's right," Melody said. "We can't let Miss Waterford do that."

"But you don't even know she is a mermaid," Howie said.

Eddie nodded toward the dirt path. Coach Waterford was jogging straight toward them. "I think it's time to prove once and for all that Coach Waterford is nothing more than a coach with big feet."

"How?" Melody asked. "You know she won't come near the water."

"Leave it to me," Eddie said. He dived under the water without even making a splash.

Coach Waterford stopped near the edge of the dock. Howie, Liza, and Melody faced her.

"Did you decide to come for a swim?" Melody asked sweetly.

Coach Waterford shook her head. "I'm just out for a run through the woods."

"Don't you ever get tired of running?" Melody asked.

Coach Waterford smiled, but she didn't get a chance to answer. Eddie popped out of the water right in front of her. With one giant splash, he sent water showering over their tall coach.

"NOOOOOO!" Coach Waterford let out an ear-piercing scream. Her eyes widened and a huge shiver shook through her arms and all the way down her long legs. Her seashell comb glowed in the sun as her feet kicked into action. Coach Waterford was a blur when she raced past Melody, Liza, and Howie.

13

Other Fish to Fry

The school bus coughed and sputtered to life as the last duffel bag was loaded.

"This has been a great track meet," Eddie said. "I hope Mr. Jenkins will make this a regular event."

"Where *is* Mr. Jenkins?" Melody asked.

"And Coach Waterford?" added Liza. "We didn't get to say good-bye."

Eddie shrugged. "I haven't seen them since we went swimming this afternoon. Let's run down to the dock. Maybe they're there."

Liza looked at her three friends. "I hope Coach Waterford didn't lure Mr. Jenkins away for good," she said softly.

Melody led the way down the dirt path. The rest of her friends jogged close behind.

The water of Lake Erin was calm. Mr. Jenkins and Coach Waterford were nowhere to be seen. Suddenly a shadow fell across them.

"I thought you kids were gone!" boomed a loud voice.

Melody, Liza, Howie, and Eddie looked up into the yellow teeth of their hairy camp counselor.

"We came to tell you good-bye," Liza explained.

"And thanks for sponsoring the track meet," Melody added.

Eddie laughed. "It was great kicking the pants off those Sheldon Sharks."

"Don't forget," Howie reminded Eddie. "Without Miss Waterford, we wouldn't have won."

"Where is Miss Waterford?" Liza asked. "We want to tell her good-bye, too."

Mr. Jenkins looked out across the lake and rubbed his whiskers. Liza was sure

she heard him sigh. "Miss Waterford is gone."

Melody put her hands on her hips. "I thought you and Miss Waterford were going to sail away together in your ship, the *Mermaid Maiden*."

Liza poked Melody as Mr. Jenkins blushed. "I thought so, too," Mr. Jenkins said.

"I'm glad you stayed," Liza told Mr. Jenkins. "Camp Lone Wolf needs you."

"But I thought the ship was your dream," Eddie blurted.

Mr. Jenkins shrugged and looked away from the water. He glanced at the woods where the birds were singing. "I think I had my dream all along, and I didn't even realize it," he said in a quiet voice. "I love these woods."

"Maybe Miss Waterford will come back," Melody suggested.

"No, I have a feeling Miss Waterford has other fish to fry," Mr. Jenkins said.

"But she did leave a note saying that this track event was the most fun she'd ever had."

The four kids watched as Mr. Jenkins walked into the woods. Liza was the first one to speak. "It's kind of sad," she said. "Miss Waterford loves to run, but she can't have her dream because she's a mermaid."

"Maybe Miss Waterford will realize she's happy with what *she* has," Howie said. "If she really is a mermaid, she belongs in the water."

"I still say you guys are crazy," Eddie teased. "Miss Waterford never was and never will be a mermaid."

Melody giggled and turned to walk back to the bus. Howie and Eddie followed her. "I guess Eddie was right," Melody agreed. "After all, mermaids don't run track."

Liza didn't say a word. She was staring at Lake Erin. While she watched, a big

tail splashed out of the water not far
from shore. Liza smiled and hurried to
catch up with her friends.

On the long bus ride back to Bailey
City, Liza never stopped smiling. And
when Howie and Eddie started singing,
Liza sang loudest of all.

About the Authors

Debbie Dadey and Marcia Thornton Jones have fun writing stories together. When they both worked at an elementary school in Lexington, Kentucky, Debbie was the school librarian and Marcia was a teacher. During their lunch break in the school cafeteria, they came up with the idea of the Bailey School Kids.

Debbie and her family live in Fort Collins, Colorado. Marcia and her husband still live in Kentucky.

Don't miss these

The BAILEY SCHOOL KIDS

Special Editions!